# Royal Blood

**Colin Anderson**

**Ukiyoto Publishing**

All global publishing rights are held by

**Ukiyoto Publishing**

Published in 2023

Content Copyright © Colin Anderson

ISBN 9789360162146

*All rights reserved.
No part of this publication may be reproduced,
transmitted, or stored in a retrieval system, in any
form by any means, electronic, mechanical,
photocopying, recording or otherwise, without the
prior permission of the publisher.*

*The moral rights of the author have been asserted.*

*This is a work of fiction. Names, characters, businesses,
places, events, locales, and incidents are either the
products of the author's imagination or used in a
fictitious manner. Any resemblance to actual persons,
living or dead, or actual events is purely coincidental.*

*This book is sold subject to the condition that it shall
not by way of trade or otherwise, be lent, resold, hired
out or otherwise circulated, without the publisher's
prior consent, in any form of binding or cover other
than that in which it is published.*

www.ukiyoto.com

*I would like to thank those who've purchased this book.
You are in for one hell of an adventure.*

# Contents

| | |
|---|---|
| Family Meeting | 1 |
| The Ways Of The Hunt | 5 |
| Becoming What You Hate | 13 |
| Royal Heritage | 15 |
| Welcome to Sanctuary | 21 |
| To Find A Cure | 26 |
| Unveiled Truth | 30 |
| Reborn | 36 |
| Two Souls... One Mind | 41 |
| The Proposal | 45 |
| Endless Hunger | 51 |
| Return to Sanctuary | 55 |

# Family Meeting

We are inside a large study with a large fireplace. They are three people within the study, two of them are men and a woman, who is sitting in a leather seat. The first man is leaning on the fireplace which is burning away, making shadows dancing on his face. Which make his glowing yellow eyes more intimidating. The other man is nursing his face.

Andre Evans

(Gruffly)

Your lucky I went easy on you, Dante . Don't EVER disrespect my daughter again.

Dante West

I was only saying she's not...

Andre Evans

That doesn't concern you, she is my daughter regardless.

Amy Evans

And he's my father, I maybe... different. But that doesn't stop me from loving him.

Dante glares at Andre as his eyes glow silver and bears his werewolf fangs. Andre returns his gaze by staring coldly. A few tense moments pass slowly as Dante backs down. Amy stands up and yawns.

Amy Evans

Now that your little pissing contest is over, I'm going for a run.

Before she can leave an elderly man with longish white hair, tied in a pony tail appears. She bows slightly and returns to her seat.

Andre Evans

Father, what brings you here?

Amy offers her seat to her grandfather, he smiles and hugs her as he gingerly sits down.

Sebastian Evans

Firstly, to end this... issue you both have. My granddaughters heritage is irrelevant. I suggest Dante that you never mention that... again, as for you Andre, control your anger.. You know what happens when you loose your... temper.

Andre Evans

I don't like those who disrespect my....

Sebastian Evans

We're ALL family Andre, it doesn't give you the right to attack your brother. Now that's cleared up, onto other matters.

Dante West

I agree with father, when is my... niece going to learn how to....

Andre Evans

She's not...

Sebastian Evans

If you two, would stop squabbling then she would find the clarity to do so. So it is my decision she will learn from myself, and this isn't up for debate. I will not force her to accompany me, if its not her wish.

Amy Evans

Sounds good to me, grandpa. I need out this house. The constant arguments and pressure to change is really fucking depressing. Not to mention pissing me off to no end.

Andre Evans

May I remind you daughter, curb your tongue. You maybe newly born, but respect your....

Sebastian Evans

Elders? Andre? If I recall, you were exactly the same when you were a cub.. But Amy has more self-confidence to speak her mind. And is willing to challenge matters, which seem immoral.

Sebastian is aided by Amy to stand and she takes his arm.

Dante West

What about us father? What will we do in the mean time?

Sebastian Evans

Like Amy's rebuttal, carry on with your pissing contest.

Amy leads her grandfather to an awaiting limousine, and opens the door for him and helps him get in, then she does the same. We watch ad it drives off, churning up the stone driveway as it does.

# The Ways Of The Hunt

Amy and her grandfather are standing inside his hallway, it's old but still wonderful. Paintings and busts, statues and gold artefacts are littered throughout. We follow as they walk into a large martial arts study.

Amy Evans

Nice study grandpa, I sense that you trained my dad in here.

Sebastian Evans

Impressive young one. Your scent tracking is more acute, than I thought. Now we begin...

Sebastian changes dramatically to his ashen coloured werewolf form. He advances on Amy. Her eyes glow emerald green and stares directly into his eyes. Sebastian begins slashing away at her, but Amy easily anticipates every move. She growls deeply at him, which stops him dead in his tracks. Amy's body smoothly changes to her werewolf form briefly, which matches the colour of her eyes. Sebastian changes back, he winces in slight pain as he retakes his human guise. He laughs hysterically while trying to catch his breath.

Sebastian Evans

Your full of surprises aren't you, nevertheless I am deeply impressed by your... form.

Amy Evans

Thanks grandpa, you words are reassuring. It... felt natural to change.

Sebastian Evans

It is rare, that one our kind can easily change the way you did. For the rest of us... it is painful, but manageable. Now we will test your ability to hunt.

We watch as she runs off and we follow before we turn and enter her fathers mansion styled house. Andre and Dante's discussion is getting heated.

Dante West

You let her go with that old dinosaur!

Andre Evans

Careful... little brother. Besides, she willingly chose to go with father. Unlike you, she respects him.

They slowly stare at each other. Then suddenly a familiar voice catches them off guard. The man enters the room wearing a worn leather jacket, sunglasses and black jeans and boots. He takes his sunglasses off and smiles showing off his blood stained fangs and his dull glowing fiery violet eyes

Dante West

You've got balls coming back here, Hunter.

Hunter Evan

What? No hug for your big brother?

Andre Evans

If father catches your scent...

Hunter Evans

That old coot? No chance, he's testing my one and only niece. Besides... I need a place to crash.

Dante West

Let me guess, you drew attention to yourself again.

Hunter Evans

You feed on one little shitty deputy, then your branded a monster.

From nowhere Sebastian in his werewolf form dramatically crashes through the window and pins hunter down while showing his fangs and growling menacingly.

Hunter Evans

(Unimpressed)

Great to see you too... Dad!

Hunter shoves him off as he retakes his human guise. Sebastian's eyes glow purple. Amy jumps through the open window and lands a heavy blow on Hunters face, which knocks him back temporarily. He chuckles heartily.

**Amy Evans**

Who's this dick grandpa?

**Sebastian Evans**

(Sighs Heavily)

This... is your uncle...

**Amy Evans**

I thought I could smell shit.

**Hunter Evans**

You've got guts kid. I like that, but doesn't mean I won't beat your ass.

**Amy Evans**

You make one move... Uncle...

**Sebastian Evans**

Enough playing around Amy... I see you've been run out another town... again. The medallion clearly didn't work.

**Andre Evans**

It was never going to work father. Clearly he ripped it off.

**Hunter Evans**

That piece of cheap shitty silver? Wasn't my style.

**Dante West**

It never was... your style. Same with the pack, according to you.

Hunter Evans

You make one mistake, and....

Sebastian Evans

Mistake hunter? MISTAKE? YOU MURDERED YOUR OWN....

Amy Evans

Murdered who?

Andre Evans

Your aunt... he claimed she was too strict.

Hunter Evans

Mother was trying to control me, I'm a werewolf...

Dante West

To live undetected with humans, we must be... discreet.

Andre Evans

For once Dante, I agree with you. We must not draw attention to ourselves.

Sebastian Evans

You speak truthfully for once Andre. To live harmoniously, and undetected we must avoid hunting them. You.. seem to not comprehend this... Hunter. That is why I must make this drastic decision.

Andre Evans

Father, I...

Amy Evans

Please grandpa! Don't...


Dante West

Please father, not this...

Sebastian Evans

Hunter... it is my decision on behalf of the circle, you are hereby banished from our clan. I also rescind your surname given to you. I must ask you to leave this house...

Hunter

Fine, you were all beginning to bore me anyway... Adios douche bags. Oh one more thing... See ya soon... Old Timer....

Hunter shoves Amy out of his way as he storms out the house. We seem him change into his werewolf form and runs off.

Dante West

Nice going father, now he'll bear a grudge that will never go away.

Andre Evans

It had to be done Dante, he was jeopardising everything. Those in a official position, such as law enforcement turn a blind eye.

The captain of the local police force barges into the study.

Captain Walker

(Gruffly)

Where is that, fucking fur ball you call your son.

Sebastian Evans

(Coldly)

Frank, do come in why don't you!

Dante and Andre slowly advance on Frank. Sebastian gestures them to back off.

Frank Walker

You don't scare me, or your family.

Amy stares at him with her bright emerald green eyes. Frank's attention is drawn to her. For a brief tense moment there is silence.

Amy Evans

(Emotionless)

Careful captain, flapping your tongue can land someone in VERY hot water. Show some decorum... please. Were not here to stroke your inflated ego...

Frank Walker

You really want to test me girl? I've already dealt with.... your kind.

Sebastian Evans

You must be thirsty Frank, please have a glass of wine... only red I'm afraid.

Frank smiles and walks over and snatches the fine crystal glass and hungrily drinks. He lets a satisfied

"Ahhh" and thrusts the empty glass back to Sebastian. He then loudly burps. All of a sudden he feels drunk.

Frank Walker

(Slurred)

Th... that wash a good... good glassh of vine. But itsh...burp... made me sheepy.

Dante Evans

Let me help you to the comfy recliner.

# Becoming What You Hate

A light breeze tickles the nose of Frank, which twitches. His new eyes snap open. He knows he's different as he stands slowly and notices he's taller. He catches his reflection in a conveniently placed mirror. He is shocked to see himself as a snow white werewolf with bright icy blue eyes. Sebastian appears behind him.

Sebastian Evans

Welcome to the family, my son

Frank Walker

(Deep Growl)

What have you done to me?

Sebastian Evans

Now you will fully comprehend, how we live. To use the upmost discretion of how we hide our... true selves from your... former race.

Amy Evans

Perhaps grandpa, he will now realize the huge struggle we face.

Frank Walker

I'll get rid of this disease, and kill every fucking one of you.

Dante changes into a crimson red werewolf with bright blue eyes. He pounces at Frank and pins him against the wall.

Dante West

(Lower Tone)

Watch your fucking mouth, cub. Or your new life will be short.

Sebastian Evans

Crescent Moon, stand down.

Dante let's him go and changes back into his human form.

Andre Evans

Snow Stalker will learn, I suspect possibly the hard way. The hunger will take hold of you. Fight as much as you want... in the end, your urge will be too strong to ignore.

Frank who is now known as Snow Stalker runs and leaps out the window. He briefly looks back. Then carries on.

# Royal Heritage

We see Amy back in her grandfather's home, she is in the study, reading a dusty old book. She flicks through the pages. She smiles as she knows who has followed her. Amy doesn't take her eyes off her book.

Amy Evans

Come to check on me dad?

Andre Evans

Your grandpa's orders. He thought seeing these... events would trouble you.

Amy gently closes the book and places it on the table., and stands in front of her father.

Amy Evans

Dad, I'm not a little pup anymore. I'm learning things I never knew. You and the rest of the family were stunned by my progress, but you didn't stop me.

Andre Evans

Yes... but your still young my child. There is so much you've still to learn.

Amy Evans

Or is it... Father... I'm learning too much for you and grandpa to handle. And your trying to hinder me.

Andre Evans

It's... not at all, but knowledge can be useful, and dangerous at the same time. We still don't understand or know your abilities, caution must be exercised at all times.

Amy Evans

I understand that, but being too cautious can make oneself paranoid and make rash decisions.

Andre Evans

You have a good head on your shoulders child, and make a valid argument. There are... certain things the circle expects of us.

Amy Evans

Isn't it my right, to find my own path. There's something about me the circle fear. Its the unknown that they don't comprehend. They know I'm very powerful, too powerful... and that's why they try to... limit where I go, and dictate where I can't.

Andre Evans

There... concerned that you'll uncover... something... you're not ready for.

Amy Evans

(Speaks in an ancient dialect)

Father, I am always ready for what destiny had set out for me.

Andre is shocked and stunned, so is her grandfather.

Sebastian Evans

Where did you... learn the language of our predecessors child. Even I cannot speak there tongue.

Andre Evans

(Irritated)

Enough of this, clearly she's been reading those... fairy tales. How convenient they were... lying around for you to find.

Sebastian Evans

(Coldly)

Careful... child! Speaking untruthfully and wild accusations will not be tolerated. My granddaughter is uncovering her own path within the circle. Her thirst for knowledge led her to the book that tells us about our predecessors ... Amy's ability to speak in there language, is clearly gifted.

Andre Evans

Not even myself or the circle, could even begin to understand there dialect. Why Amy?

A familiar voice catches all of them off guard. A older woman with white braided hair, wearing a ceremonial robe enters. They all bow, except Amy who greets her in the ancient tongue.

Amy Evans

Matriarch, the mother to all of your children, we are honoured to be in your presence


Matriarch

I haven't heard, that language in a very long time. And such manners for a youngling. You are very gifted miss Amy. Tell me, who taught you how to speak in there dialect?

Amy Evans

I was reading up on our heritage, where we came from. I then came across symbols, they didn't make sense at first... then all of a sudden they did. I understood them and was able to speak the dialect and fluently.

Andre Evans

Holy Mother, forgive my interruption but... shouldn't my daughter being taught...

Matriarch

The Hunt? But this will be very different from the way you were taught, Andre. I can see her eyes are.... unique. I believe her to be...

Andre Evans

Don't! You said that before, about....

Sebastian Evans

Mother? Are you sure of this?

Matriarch

Child, she has already proven that she can easily translate and speak there tongue. I sense that her... other unique gifts, will be further evidence.

Amy Evans

Matriarch? I unquestionably comply with your request. I will meet you at Sanctuary.

Amy easily changes to her werewolf form. They are all taken aback by her fluidity to change. She charges out of the study and the house. Once she's clear of the house, she runs very quickly that they just make her out.

Matriarch

You see me children, this is the unfathomable truth.

Andre Evans

Mother please, I beg of you...

Sebastian Evans

Child, it is alright. I know you're concerned but no harm will come to her.

The matriarch approaches Andre and places a hand tenderly on his cheek.

Matriarch

My sweet first born, she will be unharmed. I know your heart... Silent Wind,... you will always be her father... I love all of my children, including my beautiful granddaughter. Come to sanctuary and see... for yourself.

# Welcome to Sanctuary

Andre, Amy and Sebastian are standing within a old stone carven. It is lit with torches which cast dancing shadows on the walls. The matriarch is sitting on a beautiful comfortable chair. There are three other members of the circle, there faces covered.

Matriarch

My children, my fellow brothers. We are gathered within these sacred walls, to welcome into the circle my beautiful granddaughter Amy.

Amy Evans

It is my honour to be here, I'm beyond words.

Andre Evans

(Disinterested)

Being here, is a complete waste of time.

Matriarch

Child, may I remind you. That you stand with your elders, do I have to show you respect?

Andre Evans

No mother!

Sebastian Evans

Son, I love you but... I agree with the matriarch. Please show some decorum.

Amy Evans

How do we proceed my matriarch?

Matriarch

Such maturity for one who is newly born. It is clear as the moon in the night sky. Amy is the reincarnation of...

Andre Evans

NO! I WILL NOT ALLOW THIS FARCE TO...

Matriarch

YOU PETULANT CHILD, HOLD YOUR TONGUE. YOUR PETTY JEALOUSY RARES ITS HEAD AGAIN WITHIN YOU!

Andre Evans

It's...

Sebastian Evans

My son, please calm yourself.

Andre huffs and walks away and exits Sanctuary.

Matriarch

Let him have his little outburst, important matters are at hand. My dear sweet granddaughter. Do you wish to learn the ways of the hunt, according to our predecessors. Are you willing to share the blood within! And we will share our blood...

Amy Evans

(Speaks in the ancient dialect)

Matriarch, loving mother to all of your children. I humbly and willingly give my blood.

Amy walks towards her and a silver bowl rises from the floor. The matriarch is aided by the other members and walks towards the bowled well. Amy uses her fangs to pierce her skin and let a little blood into the bowl. The matriarch responds in kind. There wounds instantly heal. Amy picks up the bowl and drinks, then puts it down again.

Sebastian Evans

Another disappointment. I'm sorry....

Amy's eyes change to a bright jade green. Her appearance also changes. She is now stunningly beautiful. Her skin turns slightly white. She turns to face her grandfather.

Amy Evans

Grandpa, you have always looked out for me. As for my... Father... it seems he's been through this before. Both of you will have my protection .

Matriarch

My... ladyship...

Amy Evans

(Smiles Sweetly

Mother... there is no need for pleasantries. I'm your granddaughter... but my name will not be. My name is... Crystal Heart...

Andre makes his way back to where they're all gathered. Amy looks at him with her glowing jade green eyes. He stares at her. Not knowing it worked.

Andre Evans

(Disgusted)

What have you done... Amy are you still... you? Get out of my daughter, vile spirit

Crystal Heart

I am no vengeful spirit father. I'm still me, but things have changed. The truth has been revealed , I am Crystal Heart, first born of the circle. True matriarch, mother to all my children.

Andre Evans

Your... my mother, and my daughter.

Crystal Heart

Yes... and no. I know you grieve the loss, but I am still here. The essence of oneself remains.

Tears well in Andre's eyes.

Andre Evans

(Through clenched teeth)

You are NOT my daughter... she died the moment you were born... your nothing but an abomination.... a vile construct.

The matriarch, Sebastian and the other members advance on Andre, but Amy gestures them not to.

Crystal Heart

His heart and mind are heavy, with grief. The venomous words, spewed from his lips are from anger and loss. Pay no heed.

Andre runs out of sanctuary. Sebastian bows and changes into his werewolf form and runs off to catch him.

Matriarch

Shall I follow my lady?

Crystal Heart

No... let him grieve. Eventually he will see the truth. Nor do I hate him. No one will harm him, Make sure the other clans know this.

# To Find A Cure

Inside a abandoned lab we hear crashing and growling. We follow the noise to see snow stalker desperately searching for notes to find a way to rid himself of his lycanthropy. In his desperation he smashes important vials one including the one marked "Lycanthropy Cure". He stops to sniff the air. He looks down at the broken vial in horror. He desperately and quickly gets on the floor, lapping at the liquid, he only gets a few drops before it rapidly disappears. He is frozen in sheer terror.

Snow Stalker

(To Himself)

No... I don't want to be this... monster. Arrrgh! The hunger, its getting harder to ignore.

He suddenly catches the scent of two teenagers sneaking in to have sex. He drools uncontrollably as he is drawn to them. He tries to fight against his instinct to feed, but it over powers him.

Unbeknownst to the teens, there imminent death slowly approaches. Without warning he pounces on them. The boy screams to the girl to run. She takes off going as fast as he can. Snow Stalker stares wildly at him

Boy

Please... don't...

Snow Stalker

Kill you? Oh we're WAY past that.

He violently bites into the boys neck ripping it off alongside his bottom jaw. Blood spurts everywhere as he hungrily devours the flesh then drinks some of the boys blood, who is now dead. He wipes his mouth and begins to look for the girl. We go to where she is hiding, as snow stalker eerily calls out to her.

Snow Stalker

(Eerily Singing)

Pretty girl, I'm coming to find you.

She is frozen in sheer terror as he gets closer. He leaps over her hiding spot. And leans in to sniff her.

Snow Stalker

The smell of fear.... recognisable and... intoxicating. Isn't it.

The girl shivers in tears.

Girl

Please... I don't want to die.

Snow Stalker

Why would I let you live... human? You've nothing to offer.

Girl

I.... Will... keep your identity a secret...

Snow Stalker

Ummm..... no!

He leans in for the kill but is flung violently backwards by Andre and Dante, who begins to lands heavy bone shattering blows. Andre kneels down to the girl.

Dante

When you're far enough, yell sanctuary. Get out of here... NOW!

She runs clutching her ripped clothes, Andre looks on as she is far enough. She yells SANCTUARY. Sebastian is seen running towards the girl, he catches Andre's gaze who nods. Sebastian nods in return and gently picks up the girl and runs off.

He turns his attention to Dante, who has snow stalker pinned to the wall.

Crescent Moon

Think you can hide, Frank...

Snow Stalker

My name... is SNOW STALKER.

Night Sky

Touchy little one aren't you! But we caught your... stench!

Crescent Moon

Mother will deal with your unsanctioned hunt...... little cub.

A faint rumbling can be heard and a angry scream is faintly heard. Snow Stalker winces in pain as he changes back into his human form. He falls unconscious and at the same time Dante and Andre catch him and run off to sanctuary.

# Unveiled Truth

Amy is seen reading a old leather book in her study. She hears commotion coming from the main cavern. She changes her clothes to more ceremonial ones. And heads into the other cavern. We follow and see Frank chained to the ground. The girl is slowly recovering and shivering. Amy nods to the matriarch to take care of her. She bows and gently reassuringly helps her to her room. She turns to glare very angrily at Frank.

Crystal Heart

Thank you my sons, for bringing this so called.... castoff...

Snow Stalker

I'm no castoff bitch! I was violated by your grandpa. Turned into that... thing.

Dante West

Careful Frank, or I'll rip your fucking jaw off

Crystal Heart

Dante, son please... that won't be necessary... yet!

Andre Evans

Let me do it instead mother... I would take great pleasure...

The matriarch returns alone and bows.

Matriarch

Your highness, the girl is resting. She will eventually recover, but her wounds are deep. It will take sometime to...

Crystal Heart

Is there some of the blood left?

Matriarch

Yes but I'm not sure what it will do.

Crystal Heart

Please save her, she has been a innocent casualty.

The matriarch bows and retrieves the bowl and heads back to tend to the girl.

Snow Stalker

Shame... she would've made a tasty desert.

Crystal Heart slowly stands and walks to snow Stalker. She glares at him, her eyes glowing and she begins to chant in the ancient dialect. His body jerks violently as something is pulling at his chest. His werewolf form spirit is seen being pulled violently from him. She purifies it and sends it to where the girl is. Minutes later we hear a peaceful sigh as the girl humbly welcomes her gift.

Crystal Heart stops chanting and snow Stalker now human slumps breathing heavily. He weakly raises his head at her and smiles psychotically.

Snow Stalker

You... think this will stop me? I know everything about your... kind.

Crystal Heart

Try as you may... Frank, but you will forget once you leave sanctuary. The sense of loss and longing will cause you great sorrow, and sadness. But you will not know why. Furthermore you will find no comfort from the night...

Frank Walker

In lamens terms, I'm no longer a werewolf?

Andre Evans

(Ironically)

He's not so dumb after all!

Dante West

Brother please. Nows not the time for your sarcasm.

Crystal Heart

I agree with you my Dante. Frank Walker... formerly snow stalker... you are hereby banished from our clan... my sons, escort our... guest.

Dante and Andre grab Frank by the arms and drag him out of sanctuary. We follow as they dump in the middle of the grass fields and unchained him. They run quickly off back to sanctuary. For a brief moment Frank growls deeply, then slowly to confusion. The horror of his memory loss etched om his face.

We leave him and return to sanctuary where the girl emerges with the matriarch. She is wearing robes but modernised to trousers and crop top and her hair is short and shaved on one side and dyed light red. Her eyes glow sapphire blue.

Matriarch

My lady, she has begun a new life.

Crystal Heart

Thank you matriarch. How do you feel child.

Girl

I'm... better mother. I can't thank you enough, for saving me.

Crystal Heart

No need, it is my pleasure. You were sadly injured... but that can be discussed at a later time. Have you chosen your....

Ember Fury

I have... I am ember fury...

Crystal Heart

Sebastian, I call to you.

Sebastian slowly makes way into the cavern. He nods as he approaches.

Sebastian Evans

You called, your highness?


Crystal Heart

Yes and please call me Crystal Heart.... I wish for ember fury to learn the ways from you.

Sebastian Evans

Yes my queen.

Ember Fury

Mother, may I learn from you?

Crystal Heart

In time my child, for now you must learn from your grandpa

The two of them exit sanctuary. From the shadows Andre appears.

Andre Evans

Why did you really save her? She will eventually turn against us.

Crystal Heart

My son, I know your over protective nature wants to safeguard me and the clan. Ember Fury will not turn like your... former sibling.

Andre Evans

Just being cautious, if she shows any sign....
Crystal Heart
Trust me Andre, my sweet boy.

# Reborn

Frank sits in his small study cowering under a comfortable blanket, curled up in a ball on a soft sofa, which is lit. His eyes dart from moment to moment scanning the room, shaking uncontrollably. He temporarily breathes a sigh of relief. A voice from nowhere catches him off guard. He looks to find hunter perched on top of his book case, lying in a modelling pose. Frank is instantly terrified. Hunter peers over his sunglasses and smiles.

Frank Walker

(Nervously)

Wh... who are you?

Hunter

(Laughs Heartily)

They REALLY did a number on you didn't they, Franky boy.

Frank Walker

Le... leave my home... now!

Hunter

Calm down snowflake, if was going to kill you... I would've ripped you apart like a trash bag by now. I can help you regain what they took.


Frank Walker

Took what?

Hunter jumps down and lands near Frank and gets close to his face.

Hunter

(Excitedly)

Power... The greatest gift to be given was snatched away from you. I can help reclaim it.. The thrills, the sweet smell of fear. You can have it all back. Join me Frank, be part of my clan. Brothers in arms.

Hunter picks up a glass from a small table, pierces his skin and lets his blood flow a little. The dark viscous liquid fills the glass half way. His clawed hand, offers it to Frank. Who hesitates briefly, then guzzles it hungrily. Without warning he drops the glass and it smashes and holds his throat as he struggles for breath. He collapses heavily onto the floor.

Hunter looks on as Franks body jerks violently briefly then stops. He laughs manically as he stands back up. He turns to hunter and smiles. His eyes glow bright orange.

Hunter

Welcome back... brother... or should I say... Nightmare

Nightmare

It's good to be back, brother. I remember everything what they did... Stolen my true self, making me weak and defenceless....

Hunter

(Laughs Heartily)

That's the spirit.... Best vamoose before...

A slow clapping catches there attention. They turn to see Sebastian looking angry.

Sebastian Evans

I wouldn't put this by you. Stooping to these levels of... heresy. Mr Walker, please accompany me to...

Nightmare

(Smiles Psychotically)

My name... is nightmare, . oh don't fret... your precious sanctuary will be next.

Hunter

He knows what it takes to be truly one of us, the so called circle stick to there so called rules. We're killers in nature, why do we hide ourselves from the fleshlings!

Sebastian Evans

What gives you the right, to dictate what the circle do or act. Our interests are to ONLY hunt, when we absolutely must feed. Not of necessity... YOU... hunter... jeopardise centuries of harmonious co-existing with the humans. Those who turn a... blind eye to our little excursions are rewarded.

Nightmare

The circle are weak minded and cowards. They hide in the shadows, emerging to feed like scared cubs.

Sebastian Evans

May I remind you... hunter... you no longer are a concern us, this petty little rebellion will not play out as you think. As for you... abomination... you will fall too. I suggest you rethink what company you keep

Hunter

I see the circle are still egotistical, weak minded individuals. Hiding behind there rules, imposing limits on those who have the will to defy them. Any hint of individuality... they tighten the screws.

Sebastian Evans

You think they are rules hunter? They are merely guides left behind by our predecessors. Only a cub like yourself would think we act as strict parents. The circle exercises patience, and empathy.

Nightmare

Empathy, Ha! The circle has gone soft. They talk and talk, but very little action. The humans are cattle, and we trim the herd now and then.

Hunter

Nightmare is right, we're born to hunt, the humans are pray... and have always been... Your pissing me off, with your egotistical views, shrouded in a veil of righteousness... Now...fuck off!

Sebastian changes to his werewolf form and runs off.

Nightmare

(Angrily)

Are you fucking mad? He'll notify the circle, that I've been reborn... by you. They'll find us and either kill us, or what that bitch did.

Hunter

I know, she ripped out your wolf spirit. Trust me... I've been through it before. But I found a way back. I'm much more powerful than before . You can be too brother... the question is... how far are you willing to go?

# Two Souls... One Mind

Crystal Heart is in deep meditation as a flame like glow envelopes her. The cavern morphs to a field that glows white. Her eyes open and glow ad the flame slightly fades. She looks around and at the violet and yellow coloured sky and feels instantly at peace. Spirits of glowing blue wolves run past her. One of them stops and turns, looks at her and assumes a human guise. She looks exactly like her, except more regal, and wears tribal jewellery.

Woman

A visitor, tell me... what brings you to the great fields?

Crystal Heart

Apparently I was brought here. By who, I don't know.

Woman

I sense you have been given, the blood of your predecessors. I am the spirit of the last of your ancestors. You were given this honour centuries before you were born. To govern the clans, to be harsh but fair. To continue our... harmonious relationship with the humans.

Crystal Heart

Hunter intends to ruin everything, his delusional ideal of relying on our primal instincts.

Woman

You will deal with him, and his accomplice in due time. The other clans will need your wisdom and courage. They do not involve themselves with humanity. Believing themselves above such trivial concepts.

Crystal Heart

There is but one clan, I feel will add to our numbers. The Dawn Of Light, they have sv the same views as our clan. But I must somehow reach them.

Woman

Such noble intentions, we were right in our decision to make you our heir.

The wolves slowly gather as the woman glows in a spiritual light.

Woman

Crystal Heart, born from our noble blood. The one true matriarch, mother to all. I hereby endow you will all my power and knowledge. Take my hand child.

The woman extends her hand to Crystal Heart who tenderly takes it and the woman is absorbed into her. Her eyes glow even brighter and her appearance changes to a more regal look, imposing and stoic. The wolves bow respectfully and disappear the fields shimmer back to the cavern. Ember Fury is waiting and is relieved.

Ember Fury

Mother, I was worried. You... look... different.

Crystal Heart

I have been endowed with the last of ancestors soul.

Ember Fury

The great fields? I've heard stories about them, but never saw them.

Crystal Heart

They, my daughter are real. I am no longer Crystal Heart... I am... Mother Matriarch...

Ember Fury curtseys.

Mother Matriarch

(Smiles Sweetly)

Little one, you don't need to that. I am your mother.

The two of them exit the small cavern, and make there way into the main one.

Mother Matriarch

Children, brothers... I mother matriarch herby declare we reunite the clans. And we shall find Sebastian's home will be our home.

Once that has been established, I will journey to see the Dawn Of Light clan. And present a olive branch. To reunite our splintered brothers and sisters.

Sebastian Evans

My lady, what of hunter and his accomplice nightmare?

Mother Matriarch

In due time, they will be dealt with. They wish to attack sanctuary, and kill us. But they will find there plan... will NOT come to fruition.

# The Proposal

Mother Matriarch and Ember Fury accompanied by Sebastian are seen heading towards a Tibetan styled monastery. They approach a daunting large red wooden door, with golden rivets. They use the brass ring to announce there arrival. After several minutes of silence, the door creaks open. A man with golden eyes and orange robes greets them. Mother Matriarch bows humbly.

Man

Greetings visitors, I'm Morning Sun... pray tell... what brings thy here.

Ember Fury

(Annoyed)

That's not for you to know!

Sebastian Evans

(Whispers)

Child! Hush your tongue!

Morning Sun

It is alright my friends, young ones always speak there minds.

Mother Matriarch

I am Mother Matriarch...

Morning Sun is stunned, then regains composure, bows humbly and ushers them in. The door closes and he escorts them to the main temple.

Morning Sun

Forgive my impertinence, highness. I did not know it was you.

Sebastian Evans

It is alright brother, you didn't know.

Ember Fury

He should've!

Morning Sun

I agree. But we can discuss matters later. .

They enter the temple. Morning Sun hurries to his master, sitting in a illustrious comfortable chair. He whispers in his ear and his eyes go wide, then regains his composure. He shakes as he musters the strength to stand and shuffles towards them and speaks.

Man

Your highness, we are honoured to have you within our sacred monastery.

Mother Matriarch

The honour is mine. I thank you for your graceful hospitality... Dawn Cloud

Dawn Cloud

We are humbled by your kind words. What brings you here?

Mother Matriarch

Important matters of great urgency.

Dawn Cloud gestures to a separate room. Ember Fury and Sebastian try to follow but another member gently stops them as the door shuts. They both sit in comfortably silk chairs.

Dawn Cloud

Your grace. What is so urgent that you have travelled all this way?

Mother Matriarch

We must unite all the clans... Too long have we stayed silent. We must come together as a family.

Morning Cloud

(Frustrated)

Reunite with those.... barbarians? Out of the question. We feed only off what nature provides. We do not interfere with the world of man. We are a peaceful clan, we live in...

Mother Matriarch

Seclusion, and it is this solitary confinement has left you ignorant... of what has transpired.

Morning Cloud

Our ignorance, highness is a mask. To hide what we know what transpires. The news of your outcast of a son.... hunter has travelled far. He has turned one of the humans into one of us.

Mother Matriarch

I knew he would. He plans to kill us within sanctuary. If he does, who do you think he'll target next?

Morning Cloud

Preposterous, he will not find us.

Mother Matriarch

If I die, the last of our ancestors spirit, will flow into him, as he is a nearby host. All that knowledge and power in the hands of a relentless, emotionless killer... do you really want that to transpire?

Morning Cloud

We would discuss with him, not to attack. We are peaceful. We offer enlightenment.

Mother Matriarch

He won't care for such trivial concepts. Hunter wants power, to encourage more of our kind to join his delusional ideal of conquest.

Dawn Cloud thinks for a moment, then speaks.

Dawn Cloud

Upon further consideration, your request for our cooperation is... denied. We will not drag ourselves in to a petty squabble,


Mother Matriarch

(Angry)

You have just sealed your own death, Dawn Cloud. Not just yourself... but your entire clan. If you do reconsider, then you know where I am.

She gets up and shakes her head in disappointment as she turns and exits the room, flinging the doors open hard. Ember Fury, Sebastian and Morning Sun rush to her. They exit the temple as Dawn Cloud looks on. We follow as they make there way out of the monastery.

Morning Sun

The conversation, did not go well!

Mother Matriarch

His own arrogance, will be your downfall.

Morning Sun

Surely... he has taken on board, the ramifications of not addressing this matter. Hunter is dangerous at best, if he was gifted the spirit of our ancestor... then he would be unstoppable. Not even the might of our clans would be able to defeat him.

Ember Fury

I'll teach that fucking fool, to see sense. Even If I have to kick his ass.

Sebastian Evans

Ember Fury, that will not solve anything. Besides... he wouldn't react.

Morning Sun

I will try to convince master, to reconsider. If he fails to see reason, I will meet you at Sanctuary. May the light of our ancestors keep you safe.

# Endless Hunger

Hunter and Nightmare are within an old dank tomb. Evil looking statues glare down at them. Both of them are unfazed. They approach a ritual themed stone slab. A spiked chalice with dried blood adorns the slab. Nightmare is inexplicably drawn to it, as if it calls to him. Hunter doesn't stop him. He lifts the chalice and hungrily drinks. Minutes pass in utter silence.

Hunter

How do you feel brother?

Nightmare

(Commanding Tone)

Much.... better...

Nightmares eyes glow blood red, smiles psychotically. His fangs are very sharp looking. As he walks down the stone stairs towards hunter. He stops as he gets close to him, stares emotionless at him.

Hunter

(Sniffs)

You smell different.

Nightmare

Do I... little cub? Because I have the blood of the one, who was killed unlawfully by the ones she called family.

Hunter

Your bullshitting me! I've read the books, of our lineage... there's no mention of...

Nightmare

She was murdered for a crime she didn't commit. She argued that humans, will always be prey... and we the hunters.

Hunter

Did... she have a name?

Nightmare slowly changes to a more female figure. She moves her hands down her curves.

Ashina

Ashina is my name. Nightmare has been a most... generous host. Our interests are the same hunter. That whore, who's calls herself mother matriarch, is the direct descendant of the one who convinced the tribe to end my life.

Hunter

I thought... she was my mother.

Ashina

No my sweet child, you were born from my own womb, my blood runs through your veins. To hide you from suffering the same fate, I had to steal you away..

Hunter

(Through clenched fangs)

You...abandoned me... left me out in the fucking cold... left me to suffer. The matriarch took me in and raised me... then all of a sudden your back, and for what? To think i would have you by my side

He grabs her and leaps to a nearby wall and slams her hard against it. He stares emotionless at her. He senses the fear I'm her and sniffs and revels in it.

Ashina

My son, why do you hurt me so? I am ....

He swiftly clamps down on her lower jaw and rips it clean off, blood spewing all over him and he laps it up. He lunges into the massive wound and hungrily drinks. He lets her go. Ashina slumps to the ground, barely clinging to life as it leaves her. She looks at him remorsefully, and tries to speak but only gurgling is heard.

Hunter

Thought you'd put up more a fight. Sad really, after all your tough talk... you proved nothing. Your blood, now coursing through me will give me your soul... Then I will be unstoppable.

Ashina breathes her last, her body slumps. Her soul leaves her body, and is drawn to hunter. It tries to get away but it's too late, it is absorbed by hunter. His physique becomes more muscular and he gains a little more height, his eyes glow bright blood red. His fangs become dangerously sharp.

Hunter

(Gravely Tone)

The power, ultimate power. Coursing through my veins. No longer will I be cast aside. They will learn through suffering, that I am not to be ignored.

A deep booming voice echo's throughout the tomb.

Voice

You have desecrated this holy place, leave or be destroyed.

Hunter

Echoes, that's all you are... voices from the past, being judge on all of your descendants. This... tomb has outlasted its usefulness

Hunter runs off to the exit we follow as he does. He easily acrobats his way onto a high cliff edge to get a better vantage spot. He surveys the land below. His eyes lock onto where sanctuary is and smiles wickedly. He effortlessly leaps off the cliff and swan dives to the ground and lands gracefully, then runs to head to Sanctuary.

# Return to Sanctuary

Mother matriarch and Sebastian are talking tactics. Suddenly ember fury bursts in, her face etched with panic. They both know the look. They quickly make there way outside, to find hunter, arms crossed and eyes glowing and smiling psychotically.

Hunter

One big family reunion. Pity its short-live...

Ember Fury

Just give the word mother, and I'll teach this fucker a lesson.

Mother Matriarch

No child, he is more than a match for you. Both of you inside... now!

Sebastian nods and drags ember fury back inside sanctuary, much to her protest.

Hunter

The young, so eager... so headstrong. So dumb. I could've easily killed her but, where's the fun in that!

Mother Matriarch

I see you have cruelly twisted, my... sisters soul to your own ends.

Hunter

(Laughs Heartily)

Oh matriarch, I didn't twist anything. I simply TOOK her soul, mind you she didn't put up much of a fight. You should've seen the look on her face... when I ripped her jaw off.

Hunter tries to goat her into fighting, but she restrains herself. Without warning a bright blue blur is seen hitting hunter then quickly moving back towards mother matriarch.

Hunter grabs his jaw and reflexively rubs it, clearly annoyed at this. He gets back up to face his attacker. A bright blue werewolf wearing tribal armour, and a tattered cloak and cowl, with bright glowing white eyes stands ready to fight.

Blue Storm

(Commanding Tone)

You will not harm mother, or sanctuary... hunter

Hunter

That... voice, I know that voice... Franky boy! Alive I see, how did you survive our little encounter.

Blue Storm

I no longer go by that name, I maybe part human, but I remain in my true self. Fortunately mother found me and restored my soul and body. She then blessed me with her blood, purifying and clearing me of your disease. I awoke anew, the transgressions of what I had done, weighed heavily on me. Therefore I renounced my humanity, and became who I am now.

Hunter

BORING! Lets get this over with... you have two choices. One... you willingly give me that soul within you... Two... I kill every one of your clan, then I take your soul.

Blue Storm

You'll be dead before you even make a move.

Mother Matriarch

That won't be necessary my son. Clearly he has lost his way... deep down he doesn't want to harm me... come, let us leave... him to his thoughts.

The two of them turn and walk back to sanctuary.

Hunter

(Shouts Defiantly)

I WILL NOT BE IGNORED MATRIARCH. COME BACK AND FIGHT... BITCH! YOU WILL KNEEL AT MY FEET. EVENTUALLY I'LL

HAVE YOUR SOUL. THIS ISNT THE END BITCH

He howls in anger before running off into nearby forest, smashing trees in frustration. Screaming the words "Matriarch" over and over till his screams fade into silence.

**To Be Continued...**

www.ingramcontent.com/pod-product-compliance
Lightning Source LLC
LaVergne TN
LVHW041221080526
838199LV00082B/1870